SUPERBAT

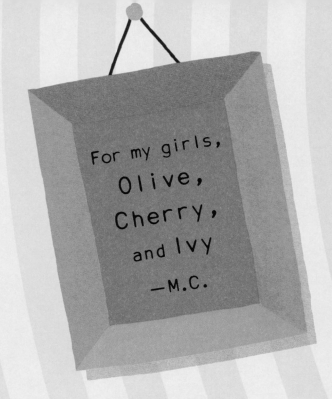

For my girls,
Olive,
Cherry,
and Ivy

—M.C.

Originally published in the United Kingdom by Scholastic, a Scholastic UK company.

ISBN 978-1-338-23003-1

10 9 8 7 6 5 4 3 2   18 19 20 21

Printed in United States of America   88
First printing 2017

SUPERBAT

MATT CARR

Scholastic Inc.

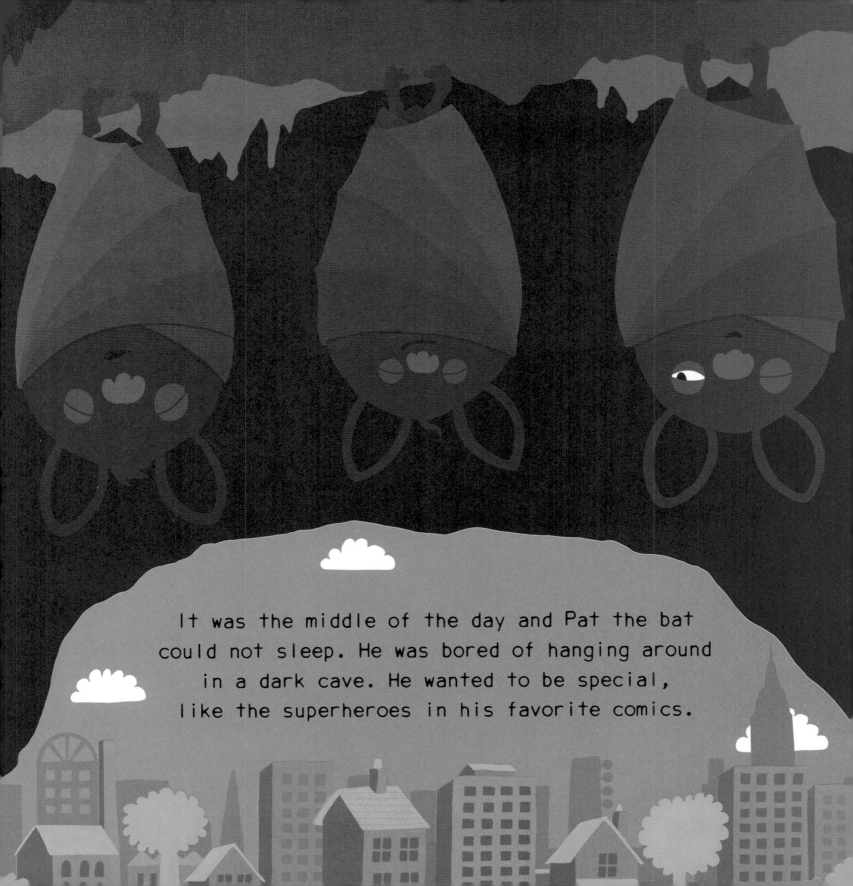

It was the middle of the day and Pat the bat
could not sleep. He was bored of hanging around
in a dark cave. He wanted to be special,
like the superheroes in his favorite comics.

And then it hit him...

POW!

Pat had a great idea and set to work.
It was not easy using Mom's sewing machine,
and his wings kept getting in the way...

but after a couple of hours, his outfit was ready.
Pat became...

When the other bats woke up, they were all surprised.
"I'm SUPERBAT!" said Pat.

"Wow," said Gary, "so what are your superpowers?"
"I have **super hearing,**" boasted Pat.

"**SO DO WE!**" his friends screeched.
"Good point," muttered Pat.

All the other bats gathered round to see SUPERBAT.

"Can you **lift a car** with your mighty muscles?" asked Gary.

"Or shoot **laser beams** from your eyes?" added Glenda.

"Well, no," said Pat, his voice wobbling a bit...

"But I can FLY!"
He leapt into the air.

"WE CAN ALL FLY!"
the other bats chuckled.
"What ELSE can you do?"

Pat tried to think of another
superskill. He felt like
every bat in town was staring
at him. He was very nervous.

"Er...I have ECHOLOCATION,
which means I can find
my way in the dark."

Pat trudged off home.
His wings drooped.
His ears flopped.
He did not feel special anymore.

"I'm just a normal bat in a silly outfit,"
he sighed, trying not to cry.

Just as Pat was about to rip off his suit and cape
and throw them away, his supersonic hearing
picked up a faint cry...

On the other side of town,
a BIG bad cat had trapped a family of mice.

Pat swooped in like a **blur** of **fur**.
The big bad cat took a...

SWAT!

But he missed
SUPERBAT.

Pat dived back down again
and flapped his wings
really fast...

WHAM!

...and scared the
mean cat away.

The mice were **free!**
"You saved us!" they cried. "Thank you!"
"But who **are** you, oh masked crusader?"

My hero!

Pat smiled modestly.
"Me? I'm no one special..."

"Oh yes you are!"
cried his bat friends, who had
followed Pat across town and
seen his heroics.

"And you DO have a
superpower: courage!
You truly ARE a...

"...SUPERBAT!"

And as Pat flew back to the bat cave for a good day's sleep,
with his friends behind him all the way,
he really did feel rather SPECIAL!

BATTY FACTS!

There are more than **1,000** types of bats. Some feed on insects, some on fruit or fish. The most well-known are VAMPIRE BATS, which feed on blood. YUCK!

Bats are **amazing!** But you don't see us often because we are **nocturnal.** That means we only come out at night!

Bats can live to a ripe old age of **twenty!**

We see in the dark using a skill called ECHOLOCATION. We make little noises and wait for the sound to bounce off things in front of us! Our **big ears** then pick up the echo, and we move out of the way!

"That's why all bats are SUPER!"